NOTRE DAME FIGHTING IRISH

BY BRIAN HOWELL

Published by ABDO Publishing Company, PO Box 398166, Minneapolis, MN 55439. Copyright © 2013 by Abdo Consulting Group, Inc. International copyrights reserved in all countries. No part of this book may be reproduced in any form without written permission from the publisher. SportsZone™ is a trademark and logo of ABDO Publishing Company.

Printed in the United States of America,
North Mankato, Minnesota
052012
092012

 THIS BOOK CONTAINS AT LEAST 10% RECYCLED MATERIALS.

Editor: Chrös McDougall
Series Designer: Craig Hinton

Photo Credits: AP Images, cover, 1, 7, 11, 17, 18, 21, 27, 29, 42 (top), 42 (bottom right), 43 (top left), 43 (top right); Bettmann/Corbis/AP Images, 4; Notre Dame/Collegiate Images/Getty Images, 8; Cal Sport Media via AP Images, 12; Harold Filan/AP Images, 23, 42 (bottom left); Toby Massey/AP Images, 24; WFH/AP Images, 30; George Gojkovich/Getty Images, 33; John Swart/AP Images, 34, 37, 43 (bottom), 44; Dave Durohik/AP Images, 39; Michael Conroy/AP Images, 41

Library of Congress Cataloging-in-Publication Data
Howell, Brian, 1974-
Notre Dame Fighting Irish / by Brian Howell.
p. cm. -- (Inside college football)
Includes index.
ISBN 978-1-61783-500-1
1. Notre Dame Fighting Irish (Football team)--History--Juvenile literature. 2. University of Notre Dame--Football--History--Juvenile literature. I. Title.
GV958.U54H68 2013
796.332'630977289--dc23

2012001856

CENTRAL ARKANSAS LIBRARY SYSTEM
CHILDREN'S LIBRARY
LITTLE ROCK, ARKANSAS

TABLE OF CONTENTS

After serving as Notre Dame's football captain, Knute Rockne became the team's legendary head coach.

ROCKNE AND THE GIPPER

KNUTE ROCKNE EVENTUALLY BECAME ONE OF THE MOST INFLUENTIAL PEOPLE IN COLLEGE FOOTBALL HISTORY. BUT HIS ARRIVAL AT NOTRE DAME'S CAMPUS IN SOUTH BEND, INDIANA, IN 1910 WAS MUCH LESS HERALDED. THE 22-YEAR-OLD FRESHMAN NEVER FINISHED HIGH SCHOOL, BUT HE WORKED FOR SEVERAL YEARS SO HE COULD SAVE MONEY FOR COLLEGE. ROCKNE WAS SMALL, STANDING JUST 5 FEET 8 INCHES TALL AND WEIGHING 160 POUNDS.

However, he became a valuable member of the Fighting Irish football team for four years. Rockne was the team captain in 1913. He was also an All-American in 1913. Notre Dame went 24–1–3 during his four seasons.

Rockne and quarterback Charles "Gus" Dorais dazzled opponents. Before they came along, few college teams used the forward pass. It became a bigger weapon during those years. Dorais and Rockne were the best, though. Dorais threw the ball and Rockne caught it.

HISTORY OF SUCCESS

Throughout college football history, few teams can match the success Notre Dame has had on the field. Going into the 2012 season, just two schools had won more games than Notre Dame's 853. They were Michigan (895) and Texas (857). The Irish had a winning percentage of .731. That was barely second to Michigan (.736). Notre Dame also had 11 national championships and 80 All-American players. That was more than any other school.

Rockne was involved in a little bit of everything during his time as a student at Notre Dame. The Norway native wrote for the student yearbook and the newspaper. He was a part of the school orchestra, too, playing the flute. He played a major role in student plays. And he even got to the finals at a Notre Dame marbles tournament. Rockne was also an exceptional student who graduated with honors while studying chemistry.

It was coaching that gained Rockne his most fame, though. After graduating, he served as an assistant coach for four years under coach Jesse Harper. Then Rockne was named head coach in 1918. Rockne led the Fighting Irish for 13 years, from 1918 to 1930. He is still considered one of the best college football coaches of all time.

Rockne was a great motivator. He also designed some of the team's equipment. In addition, Rockne was the first coach to take his team around the country to play other teams. Most teams just played opponents located near to them to save money. Notre Dame did play

Notre Dame coach Knute Rockne, *left*, instructs a player during practice in 1925. That team finished 7–2–1.

other Indiana teams. But the Fighting Irish also traveled coast to coast, from New York to Los Angeles.

On the field, Rockne's teams were often among the country's best. He won 88 percent of his games. Through 2011, that was still the best winning percentage for any college or professional football coach. In all, Notre Dame had 105 wins, 12 losses, and five ties during Rockne's 13 years. In five of his 13 seasons, Rockne led Notre Dame to an undefeated record. And the Irish were crowned national champions three times with Rockne—in 1924, 1929, and 1930.

Notre Dame's George Gipp was a top all-around football player. He rushed, passed, punted, and even played defensive back.

During his time at Notre Dame, Rockne coached some of the most famous players in college football history. Among them was George "The Gipper" Gipp. It is generally believed that Rockne discovered Gipp while Rockne was still an assistant coach. Like Rockne, Gipp did not finish high school. Gipp also came to Notre Dame as an older freshman. Arriving in 1916, Gipp came to South Bend to play baseball. One day, Rockne saw Gipp drop-kicking a football for fun. Seeing the talent in the freshman, Rockne invited Gipp to try out for football.

Gipp was not the easiest player to manage. He liked the nightlife much more than he liked school. He often was late for practices—or did not show up at all. But when Gipp got on the field, he had few peers. By the time he was a senior in 1920, he was considered the best player in college football.

"I felt the thrill that comes to every coach when he knows it is his fate and his responsibility to handle unusual greatness . . . the perfect performer who comes rarely more than once in a generation," Rockne said of Gipp. "He was a natural athlete. . . . And he possessed the three most important qualities needed to attain greatness: the qualities of body, mind, and spirit. He had what no coach or system can teach—football intuition."

WIN ONE FOR THE GIPPER

Perhaps the most famous speech in sports history came from Knute Rockne. On November 10, 1928, Rockne's struggling Notre Dame team was preparing to face the favored Army team. George Gipp had died nearly eight years earlier. But according to Rockne, Gipp gave Rockne one final wish when he was dying.

To rally his team, Rockne delivered Gipp's words: "Some time, Rock, when the team is up against it, when things are wrong and the breaks are beating the boys—tell them to go in there with all they've got and win just one for the Gipper. I don't know where I'll be then, Rock. But I'll know about it. And I'll be happy."

The speech worked. Notre Dame took the field at Yankee Stadium in New York that day and upset Army 12–6.

Extremely athletic, Gipp could do it all. He led Notre Dame in rushing and passing during his final three seasons. He was a great punter. And he also was one of the best defensive backs the Irish have ever had. Through the 2011 season, Gipp still held a few Notre Dame records.

Rockne and Gipp both had a tremendous impact on Notre Dame football—and on college football, in general. Both of their lives ended in tragedy, too.

During Gipp's senior season, he became ill with strep throat. That led to him getting pneumonia. He never recovered. On December 14, 1920—just 24 days after his last game—Gipp died. He was just 25 years old. Gipp's death was mourned around the country, and especially in South Bend and his hometown of Laurium, Michigan.

Nearly 11 years later, tragedy again struck Notre Dame. On March 31, 1931, Rockne got on an airplane bound for Los Angeles. He was going there for a meeting about a football-themed movie. Shortly after takeoff, the plane flew into a storm. It crashed near Emporia, Kansas. All eight people on the plane died. Rockne had turned 43 earlier that month.

ON THE BIG SCREEN

The 1940 movie *Knute Rockne All-American* portrayed the life of the legendary coach, played by actor Pat O'Brien. The movie included a scene in which George Gipp—played by future US President Ronald Reagan—gave his last dying wish to Rockne.

Future US President Ronald Reagan, *center*, played George Gipp in the famous 1940 movie *Knute Rockne All-American*.

From 1910 to 1930, either Rockne or Gipp—or both—were a part of Notre Dame football. During those seasons, the Fighting Irish had a remarkable record of 156 wins, 18 losses, and 9 ties. They had eight undefeated seasons and three national titles in those years.

Several legendary players and coaches have led the Irish to national championships in the decades that followed. Yet, the legends of Rockne and Gipp are far from forgotten. They are still considered two of the greatest men to ever lead the Irish.

The famous "Touchdown Jesus" mural is painted on Hesburgh Library near Notre Dame Stadium.

THE FOUR HORSEMEN

TODAY, MICHIGAN AND NOTRE DAME ARE BITTER RIVALS. THEY HAVE PLAYED EACH OTHER NEARLY EVERY YEAR SINCE 1978. IN FACT, NOTRE DAME'S FIRST-EVER FOOTBALL GAME WAS AGAINST MICHIGAN ON NOVEMBER 23, 1887. HOWEVER, THE WOLVERINES CAME TO SOUTH BEND TO DO MORE THAN PLAY FOOTBALL. THEY ALSO CAME TO TEACH NOTRE DAME *HOW* TO PLAY FOOTBALL.

Michigan won that game 8–0. Football in its early days hardly resembled the game played today. By most accounts, it was more similar to rugby than modern football. Yet by 1924, Notre Dame was firmly established as one of the top college teams in the country.

The Irish finished with zero or one loss in 17 of 18 seasons between 1906 and 1923. Their worst record in those years was a 6–2 mark in 1914. The 1924 season, however, would go down as one of the greatest in school history. That year, the Irish won their first consensus national title. It came thanks in large part to a quartet of star players.

Jim Crowley, Elmer Layden, Don Miller, and Harry Stuhldreher were seniors on the 1924 team. They made up the Notre Dame backfield under coach Knute Rockne. Individually, each one of them was a great player.

Crowley was a great runner and kicker. He led the Irish in scoring in 1924. Layden was faster than the other three. In addition to his running, Layden was the team's top kick returner. Stuhldreher was Notre Dame's quarterback, and he also returned punts. And in his career, Miller had more rushing yards than every player in Notre Dame history to that point except for one—the legendary George Gipp. Miller was the team's top runner and receiver in 1924.

Each one of those four players is enshrined in the College Football Hall of Fame. Together, they are forever known as the Four Horsemen.

BACK-TO-BACK CHAMPIONS

The 1924 season was the first national championship season for Notre Dame. The Irish would go on to win two more under coach Knute Rockne. In 1929, All-Americans Frank Carideo and Jack Cannon led the Irish to a 9–0 record. The next season, Carideo and Marchy Schwartz were two of the team's best players in a 10–0 season. The Irish were crowned national champions after both seasons.

During that 19-game stretch, Notre Dame outscored its opponents 410–112. Carideo, Cannon, and Schwartz have all been inducted into the College Football Hall of Fame. Three other Hall of Famers also were a part of at least one of those two championship teams: Frank Hoffmann, Bert Metzger, and Tommy Yarr.

In 1924, the Four Horsemen led Notre Dame to a 10–0 record and the school's first national championship. The key win that season—and the key moment in the legend of the Four Horsemen—came on October 18, 1924, at the Polo Grounds in New York. That day, Notre Dame played the powerful Army team. Layden scored a touchdown in the first half. Crowley added another one in the second half. And Notre Dame went on to win 13–7. It was Army's only loss all season.

After the game, famous sportswriter Grantland Rice wrote about it for the *New York Herald-Tribune*. The lead of his story is still considered one of the greatest pieces of work in sports journalism history:

"Outlined against a blue-gray October sky, the Four Horsemen rode again," he wrote. "In dramatic lore they are known as Famine, Pestilence, Destruction, and Death. These are only aliases. Their real names are Stuhldreher, Miller, Crowley, and Layden. They formed the crest of the South Bend cyclone before which another fighting Army football team was swept over the precipice at the Polo Grounds yesterday afternoon as 55,000 spectators peered down on the bewildering panorama spread on the green plain below."

He later added: "Yesterday the cyclone struck again as Notre Dame beat the Army, 13 to 7, with a set of backfield stars that ripped and crashed through a strong Army defense with more speed and power than the warring cadets could meet."

Shortly after that game, Notre Dame student publicity aide George Strickler had an idea. He got the four players to pose in uniform while sitting atop horses. The photo is still one of the most famous in sports history.

Notre Dame was selected to play in the Rose Bowl after that season, on January 1, 1925. The Rose Bowl was the first bowl game, and it remains among the most important. In that 1925 game, the Irish defeated Stanford 27–10. That win clinched the national championship. However, it was the first—and only—bowl game in which the Irish played before 1969.

From 1922 through 1924, the Four Horsemen dominated Notre Dame opponents. But it was on that October day against Army that they became legendary.

None of the Four Horsemen was taller than 6 feet. None weighed more than 165 pounds, either. Yet, nearly a century later, they remain among the giants in college football history. Together they played 30 games, going 27–2–1. The only team to beat them was Nebraska, which did so twice.

NOTRE DAME STADIUM

On October 4, 1930, the Irish opened Notre Dame Stadium. Marchy Schwartz scored the game-winning touchdown with four minutes to play in that inaugural game. The score lifted the Irish past Southern Methodist University (SMU) 20–14. In 1930, the stadium cost $750,000 to build. About $50 million was then spent in 1997 to expand the stadium, which now seats more than 80,000 fans. Since 1966, all but one game—on Thanksgiving Day in 1973 against Air Force—has been a sellout.

Notre Dame's Four Horsemen pose on horses in this famous photo following the 1924 game against Army.

Following their playing careers, the Four Horsemen all went into coaching. Layden actually coached the Irish to a 47–13–3 record from 1934 to 1940. One of those wins came at Ohio State on November 2, 1935. Notre Dame scored with 32 seconds left to upset the Buckeyes 18–13. It was one of the most famous games of its time.

From its humble beginnings in 1887 through 1930, Notre Dame played some great football and had some great players. Nothing, however, could compare to the Four Horsemen and the 1924 national championship squad.

Linebacker Jerry Groom intercepted a pass against SMU to seal Notre Dame's 1949 national championship.

3

THE LEGEND CONTINUES

NOTRE DAME HAD THE BEST TEAM IN COLLEGE FOOTBALL IN 1949. ON THE FINAL DAY OF THE SEASON, HOWEVER, THE IRISH FOUND THEMSELVES IN A BATTLE. NOTRE DAME HAD A 27–20 LEAD AGAINST THE SMU MUSTANGS ON DECEMBER 3, 1949. TIME WAS RUNNING OUT, BUT SMU QUARTERBACK KYLE ROTE HAD HIS TEAM IN POSITION FOR A GREAT UPSET.

Rote and the Mustangs had marched all the way down the field. Now they were just a couple of feet from a game-tying touchdown. With time for one more play, Rote tried a jump pass into the end zone. Instead of an SMU receiver, the ball landed in the hands of Notre Dame junior linebacker Jerry Groom. That gave Notre Dame the win—and another national title. It also capped off one of the greatest decades in college football history.

Notre Dame was usually one of the country's best teams. But in the 1940s, under the direction of coach Frank Leahy, the Irish were nearly unstoppable. Leahy had great success

FIRST HEISMAN

In 1943, quarterback Angelo Bertelli helped Notre Dame win the national title and became the first Heisman Trophy winner in school history. He played in just six games but threw for more than 500 yards and 10 touchdowns. Then Bertelli left to serve in the Marines during World War II. Later that year, he was going through boot camp in Parris Island, South Carolina, when he listened on the radio to Notre Dame's upset loss against Great Lakes. "I left the room crying and when I went outside, that's when I was handed the telegram that I had won the Heisman," he said.

on the football field. That should not be a surprise, since he grew up in Winner, South Dakota. Leahy played tackle at Notre Dame from 1928 to 1930. As a player, he won two national titles under coach Knute Rockne. And in 1941, Leahy became Notre Dame's head coach.

Leahy had instant success. He went 8–0–1 in his first season. In his third season, he led the Irish to the 1943 national title with a 9–1–0 record. Leahy missed the next two seasons as he served in the US Navy during World War II. But he resumed his position as Notre Dame head coach in 1946. Starting that season, the Irish went four straight years without losing a game. From 1946 to 1949, they went 36–0–2 and won three national championships.

Quarterback John Lujack won the 1947 Heisman Trophy as college football's best player. Lujack was the second Irish player to win the award after Angelo Bertelli won in 1943. Lujack led the Irish to the 1946 and 1947 national titles along with All-American tackle George Connor.

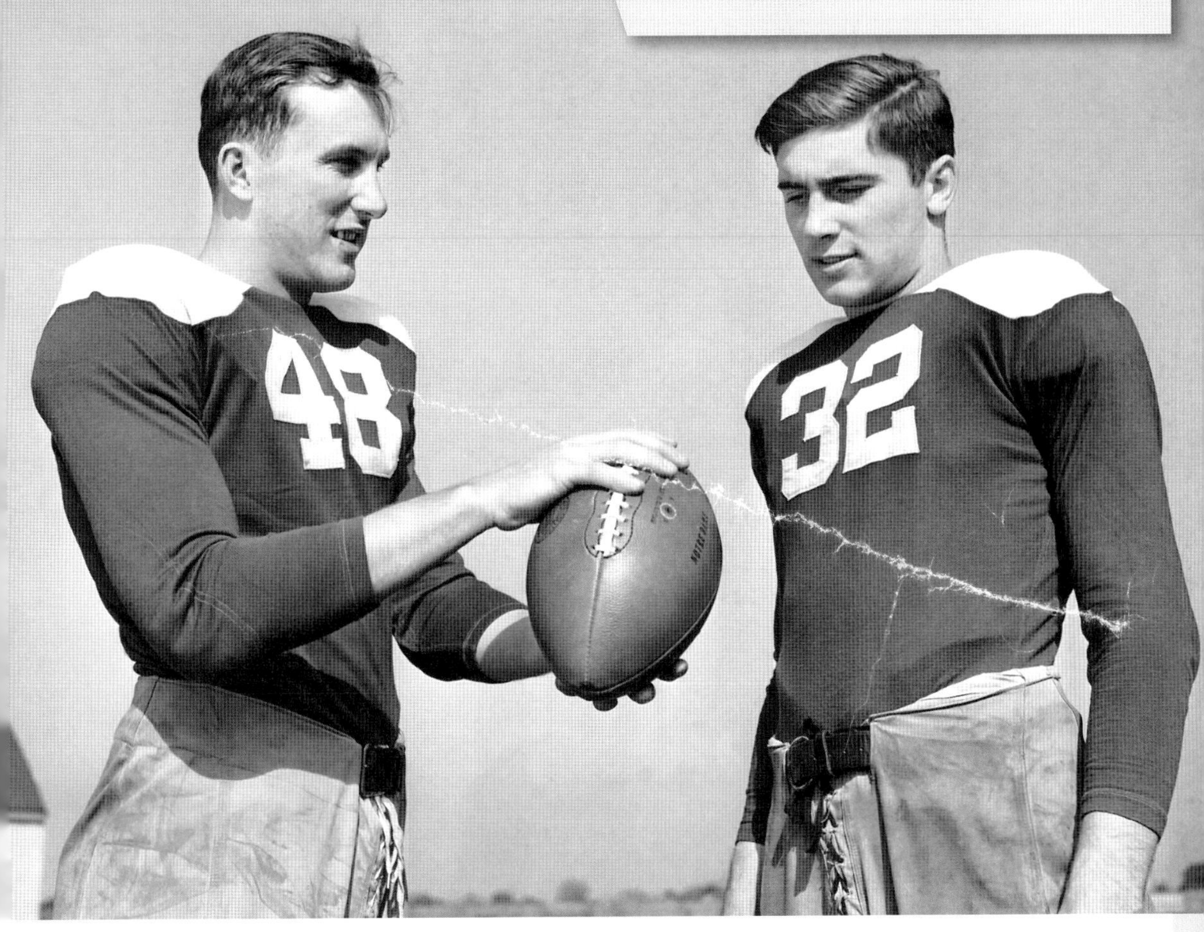

Angelo Bertelli, *left*, and John Lujack are considered two of Notre Dame's greatest quarterbacks.

The last of those titles was won in 1949, when Notre Dame beat SMU. The Irish finished the season 10–0. All-Americans Emil Sitko, Jim Martin, Bob Williams, and Leon Hart led the team. Hart won that year's Heisman Trophy.

"This is the greatest team I ever coached," Leahy said of the 1949 team. "Don't you think it must be the finest we have had at Notre Dame?"

As great as the 1949 team was, Leahy knew many of his best players were graduating. Shortly after beating SMU, he said, "We will lose five games next year." He was almost right. The Irish went 4–4–1 in 1950.

The losing did not last long, though. Notre Dame was able to add more talented players over the next couple years. By 1953, Leahy and the Irish finished 9–0–1 and ranked second in the nation. That was his last season, however. And tough times were ahead.

From 1954 to 1963, three men took turns as Notre Dame's coach. The Irish went 51–48 during those 10 seasons. From 1889 to 1955, the Irish had only had one losing season. They then had three from 1956 to 1963. One of the most memorable games during those years came on November 16, 1957. That day, the Fighting Irish visited top-ranked Oklahoma. The Sooners had won 47 games in a row—a record that still stood as of 2012. On this day, however, Notre Dame came out on top and ended Oklahoma's winning streak. Dick Lynch scored the only touchdown in a 7–0 victory.

GOLDEN BOY WINS HEISMAN

There was not much Paul Hornung could not do. Hornung, nicknamed the "golden boy," had his best season in 1956. That season, he led Notre Dame in rushing, passing, scoring, and return yards. In addition to running and throwing, he kicked the ball and played defense. As great as he was, though, the Irish won just two of their 10 games. Still, Hornung was recognized as the Heisman Trophy winner. Through 2011, he was still the only player from a losing team to win the award. After college, Hornung had a Hall of Fame career with the National Football League's (NFL's) Green Bay Packers.

Notre Dame's Heisman Trophy-winning quarterback Paul Hornung runs during a 1956 game against Southern California.

Eventually, the glory days would return to Notre Dame. But nothing could match the run of success that Leahy and his teams had in the 1940s.

Notre Dame coach Ara Parseghian talks with quarterback Terry Hanratty on the sidelines during a 1967 game.

4

KEEPING WITH TRADITION

ARA PARSEGHIAN WAS DIFFERENT FROM EVERY OTHER NOTRE DAME COACH BEFORE HIM. PARSEGHIAN WAS THE FIRST NOTRE DAME COACH WHO HAD NOT PLAYED FOR THE IRISH. HE WAS ALSO THE FIRST NOTRE DAME COACH WHO WAS NOT CATHOLIC. NOTRE DAME IS A CATHOLIC SCHOOL. STILL, THE FOOTBALL TEAM NEEDED A BOOST. AND IT TURNED OUT THAT PARSEGHIAN WAS THE MAN FOR THE JOB.

Notre Dame hired Parseghian following a disappointing 2–7 season in 1963. The school hoped he could restore the winning tradition. It did not take long for Parseghian to prove he belonged in the Notre Dame coaching fraternity. In his first season, Parseghian led the Irish to a 9–1 record and a number three national ranking. By his third year, the Fighting Irish again were national champions.

Perhaps the biggest game in Parseghian's 11 years at Notre Dame did not result in a win, but a tie. On November 19, 1966, the top-ranked Irish visited second-ranked Michigan State.

HUARTE'S HEISMAN

Of the seven Notre Dame players to win a Heisman Trophy through 2011, none were as surprising as John Huarte. He rarely played before his senior season in 1964. And as a junior, he was the third-string quarterback. Ara Parseghian made Huarte the starter in Parseghian's first season. The California native shined. Huarte set 12 school records that season and led the Irish to a 9–1 record. Senior wide receiver Jack Snow finished fifth in Heisman balloting. It was one of four times the Irish have had two players in the top five.

More than 80,000 fans filled Spartan Stadium in East Lansing, Michigan. Another 33 million watched on television.

Michigan State jumped out to a 10–0 lead. Just before halftime, sophomore running back Bob Gladieux scored a touchdown for Notre Dame. Then on the first play of the fourth quarter, Irish junior kicker Joe Azzaro booted a field goal. That tied the game at 10–10.

The game was still tied when Notre Dame got the ball back with 1:24 left to play. Several of Notre Dame's best players were injured by that point. Also, a tough wind was whipping through the stadium. With those things in mind, Parseghian made the decision to run the ball several times to run out the clock. The game ended in a 10–10 tie. Many people questioned his decision to not go for the win. However, the Irish came out the next week and crushed the University of Southern California 51–0. That secured the Irish's first national championship in 17 years.

"That was one of the most beautiful football games that has ever been played," Parseghian said after the tie with Michigan State. "What

Notre Dame running back Bob Gladieux dives over Southern California defenders during a 1968 game.

the writers and the general public wanted was a winner out of this ballgame. The strategy that we employed is one that I have absolutely no regret about."

All-Americans Nick Eddy, Jim Lynch, Tom Regner, and Alan Page led that 1966 squad. More than 12 Notre Dame players earned some sort of All-America recognition that year. That was more than in any other year in school history. It was one of the most dominating Notre Dame teams ever. That season, the Irish outscored their 10 opponents 362–38. Six teams failed to score a single point on the Irish defense.

The 1969 and 1970 squads did not win national titles. They did get to bowl games, though. Notre Dame's only bowl appearance up to that point was the Rose Bowl after the 1924 season. Led by star quarterback Joe Theismann, the Irish went to the Cotton Bowl after the 1969 and 1970 seasons. Notre Dame played Texas in both games. And Texas entered each game ranked number one.

The Longhorns won the first battle 21–17. In the second, Theismann led the Irish to a 24–11 upset win in his final game. Theismann threw for 176 yards and a touchdown. He also ran for two touchdowns. Notre Dame finished 10–1 and ranked number two in the country. Theismann went on to a stellar professional career. He led the NFL's Washington Redskins to a Super Bowl win in 1983.

The Irish had just two All-Americans in 1973. They were senior tight end Dave Casper and senior defensive back Mike Townsend. Still, Notre Dame won another national championship that fall. That 1973 team had the fewest All-Americans of any of Notre Dame's 11 national championship teams.

Yet behind Casper, Townsend, and junior quarterback Tom Clements, Notre Dame finished 11–0. They wrapped up the championship with a 24–23 win over Alabama in the Sugar Bowl.

Parseghian coached one more year in South Bend before retiring. He had an 11-year record of 95–17–4. His Irish teams won two national titles and finished ranked in the top 10 nine times. For that, he was inducted into the College Football Hall of Fame in 1980.

To replace Parseghian, Notre Dame hired Dan Devine. Devine had previously coached at Arizona State, Missouri, and for the Green Bay

Notre Dame quarterback Joe Theismann runs with the ball during a 1970 game against Purdue.

Packers of the NFL. His task was simple: keep winning. And he did. In six years with Devine, the Irish went 53–16–1. That included an 11–1 record and another national championship in 1977.

Notre Dame's prospects did not always look bright in 1977. The Irish lost their second game of the year 20–13 to Mississippi. That dropped them to number 11 in the national rankings. But the Irish came back to win their last nine regular-season games. Now ranked fifth, they faced top-ranked Texas in the Cotton Bowl on January 2, 1978.

Texas was the only unbeaten team in major college football. Yet prior to the game, Notre Dame junior linebacker Bob Golic made a bold prediction. "I think we are going to beat them soundly," he said. "In my opinion, it won't be a squeaker."

Notre Dame quarterback Joe Montana and coach Dan Devine led the Fighting Irish to the 1977 national title.

Notre Dame's defense was spectacular in 1977. In addition to Golic, the Irish featured senior defensive end Ross Browner. Some consider Browner to be the best defensive player in Notre Dame history. But Texas' powerful running back Earl Campbell had won the Heisman Trophy that year. Behind Campbell, Texas had one of the top offenses in the country that season.

In the Cotton Bowl, Notre Dame's defense won the battle. Campbell had a good day. But the Longhorns had six turnovers.

Notre Dame's offense had some stars of its own. Junior quarterback Joe Montana would go on to a Hall of Fame career while leading the San Francisco 49ers to four Super Bowl titles. Senior tight end Ken MacAfee was an All-American. Irish running backs junior Jerome Heavens (101 yards) and sophomore Vagas Ferguson (100 yards) both ran well against Texas. Ferguson scored three touchdowns. Montana threw for 111 yards and a touchdown.

When it was over, Notre Dame had won 38–10. That gave the Irish their tenth national title. Golic was named the game's Most Valuable Player on defense. "I just had to remind coach," Golic said, "that I was right all along."

Montana did not have his best day in the national title game. And he never did earn All-American honors. Yet it was at Notre Dame that he first became a legend. Perhaps his greatest individual moment for the Irish came in his last college game.

RUDY!

One of the most famous players in Notre Dame history hardly ever played for the Irish. Daniel "Rudy" Ruettiger came from a large family in Joliet, Illinois. He grew up watching Notre Dame football and dreamed of one day playing for the Irish. Rudy was a good player in high school. However, most college coaches considered him to be too small to play at that level. In addition, Rudy did not initially get into Notre Dame.

After two years of hard work at nearby Holy Cross, Rudy eventually got accepted into Notre Dame. He managed to make the football team as a practice player in 1974 and 1975. Finally, in the last home game of the 1975 season, Rudy was allowed to dress in uniform. In the last minute of a 24–3 win over Georgia Tech, Rudy got to play for the first—and only—time. His story was told in a 1993 movie called *Rudy.*

On January 1, 1979, Notre Dame played Houston in the Cotton Bowl. It started out as a miserable day. The weather was horrible, and so was Montana's play. He was sick with the flu. Montana nearly did not play the second half. But thanks to some chicken soup, he started feeling better and went back to the field late in the third quarter. The game came down to its final play. That is when Montana threw a touchdown pass to Kris Haines to give the Irish a 35–34 win.

Devine resigned after the 1980 season to spend more time with his wife, who had become ill. "In 33 years I've never had a team quit on me and they did not quit today," Devine said after his last game, a 17–10 loss to top-ranked Georgia in the Sugar Bowl. "I think any coach who can get through 33 years and not have that happen is very, very fortunate."

Gerry Faust was named as Devine's replacement. As always, the Irish players looked forward to a bright future. "I think since we're so young we've got excellent [players] coming back and I think we're looking forward to some great years ahead," said freshman quarterback Blair Kiel.

Unfortunately for Kiel and the Irish, the Faust years did not turn out as hoped. But as usual, great players came through South Bend. Among

PINKETT RACKS UP YARDS

From 1982 to 1985, Allen Pinkett was a star running back for the Irish. He ended his college career as the school's all-time leader in rushing yards with 4,131. His 1,394 yards in 1983 has remained one of the best single-season totals in team history through 2011. He is also one of just two players in school history with three 1,000-yard seasons.

Notre Dame quarterback Blair Kiel prepares to take the snap during a 1982 game against Pittsburgh.

them were All-American linebacker Bob Crable, defensive back Dave Duerson, and running back Allen Pinkett. And Faust ended up with a winning record of 30–26–1 in his five seasons. However, the Irish never won more than seven games in a single season with Faust. In his last year, 1985, Notre Dame began the season ranked fourteenth in the country. With three straight losses to close the season, the Irish finished just 5–6. Lou Holtz then replaced Faust after the 1985 season. Notre Dame's fortunes finally started looking brighter after that.

Behind quarterback Tony Rice, Notre Dame's 1988 team was known as one of the best Fighting Irish squads ever.

UPS AND DOWNS

IT DID NOT TAKE LONG FOR LOU HOLTZ TO RETURN NOTRE DAME TO ELITE STATUS. THE IRISH WENT JUST 5–6 IN HIS FIRST SEASON IN 1986. BUT THEY STARTED THE NEXT SEASON 8–1 BEFORE ULTIMATELY LOSING THEIR FINAL THREE GAMES.

Heading into the 1988 season, Notre Dame was ranked among the top 15 teams in the country. Before long, the Irish were in the top five. And by the end of the year, the 1988 squad was being called one of the greatest Notre Dame teams ever.

Led by dual threat junior quarterback Tony Rice, Notre Dame went 12–0. Rice led the Irish in passing and rushing in both 1988 and 1989. He also benefited from running behind All-American senior tackle Andy Heck. Notre Dame featured four All-Americans on defense as well.

Another emerging star that season was Raghib "The Rocket" Ismail. The freshman wide receiver led the country in kickoff return average that season. He also returned two kicks for touchdowns in a blowout win against Rice University.

All that talent guided Notre Dame to perfection, although it had a couple of close calls. The Irish needed a late push to beat Michigan in the opener. Then in October, they upset top-ranked Miami 31–30.

Miami drilled the Irish in their previous four meetings. On this day, though, Notre Dame jumped to a 21–7 lead. The Irish had the lead when Miami scored a touchdown with 45 seconds to play. That made it 31–30 in favor of Notre Dame. Miami decided to go for a two-point conversion after the touchdown. But the pass was incomplete and Notre Dame held on to win.

The Irish dominated all of their other opponents that season. And when they beat third-ranked West Virginia 34–21 in the Fiesta Bowl, the Irish captured their eleventh national championship.

BROWN CAPTURES HEISMAN

Notre Dame has had seven Heisman Trophy winners through 2011. However, an Irish player had won the trophy only once since 1964. In 1987, senior Tim Brown was sensational for the Irish. Brown was a great receiver and kick returner. He actually had a better year, statistically, in 1986. But in 1987, he was sixth in the country with 167.9 all-purpose yards per game. He easily won the Heisman voting and was elected to the College Football Hall of Fame in 2009.

"Mom, I know you wanted me to be in the band," Brown said during his Heisman Trophy speech, "and dad, I know you wanted me to play football. I wanted to do both, but I had to make a choice. Mom, I hope you're not disappointed with my choice." Following college, Brown had a successful NFL career as a receiver playing mostly with the Los Angeles/Oakland Raiders.

Notre Dame running back Ricky Watters runs against Navy in 1989. He had 134 yards on nine carries in the Irish win.

That was Notre Dame's last national title through 2011. However, the school had several great teams after that. The 1989 team, in fact, looked poised to win another title. Notre Dame opened the year at number two. It then jumped to number one after beating Virginia to open the season. The Irish stayed atop the rankings for the next two months. They were 11–0 going into the final regular-season game. However, this time it was Miami that pulled the upset. The seventh-ranked Hurricanes won 27–10. Miami finished the season ranked number one, while Notre Dame was number two.

ROCKET ROBBED?

Many Irish fans believed Raghib "The Rocket" Ismail should have won the Heisman Trophy in 1990. Ismail was a great receiver who also electrified the crowd with his punt and kick returns. He is the only player in college football history through 2011 to score touchdowns on two kickoff returns in two separate games. He finished as runner-up in the 1990 Heisman Trophy voting to Brigham Young University quarterback Ty Detmer.

Quarterback Rick Mirer and running backs Reggie Brooks and Jerome Bettis led a powerful Irish offense in the early 1990s. Mirer was a top quarterback. Brooks ran for over 1,300 yards in 1992. And Bettis, who was a big, bruising running back, ran for 825 yards that season. Bettis wound up being the biggest star of the three. He finished his 13-year NFL career as the fifth-leading rusher in league history.

Notre Dame went 10–1–1 in 1992. And it was even better in 1993. That year, the Irish went 11–1, and barely lost the one. The 1993 season also produced two of the most amazing finishes in school history.

The second-ranked Irish hosted top-ranked Florida State on November 13. Heisman Trophy-winning quarterback Charlie Ward led Florida State. With three seconds left, Ward and the Seminoles had the ball at Notre Dame's 14-yard line. However, sophomore safety Shawn Wooden batted down Ward's next pass. That gave Notre Dame a 31–24 win and the number-one ranking.

But Notre Dame's national title hopes were dashed just one week later. Catholic school rival Boston College came to South Bend.

Notre Dame running back Jerome Bettis runs into the end zone during a 1992 game against Penn State.

The seventeenth-ranked Eagles led 38–17 at one point. Notre Dame stormed back to take a 39–38 lead. However, Boston College kicker David Gordon booted a 41-yard field goal on the last play of the game. The Eagles won 41–39.

Florida State and Notre Dame both finished with one loss. Holtz and the Irish argued they should be the champion because they beat Florida State. However, the Seminoles wound up winning the title.

Holtz coached three more years with the Irish. He left with a record of 100–30–2. Knute Rockne, with 105 wins, was the only Notre Dame coach with more wins than Holtz through 2011. The Irish have had ups and downs since Holtz left in 1996.

Bob Davie replaced Holtz. He led the team to three winning seasons but was fired after a disappointing 5–6 season in 2001. In 2002, Tyrone Willingham became the first African-American head coach in Notre Dame history. The Irish went 10–3 in his first season. However, they went a combined 11–12 in the two years with Willingham after that. He was fired before the final game in 2004.

Charlie Weis then took over in 2005. Star quarterback Brady Quinn led the Irish in Weis's first two seasons. Quinn finished his career in 2006 with the most passing yards (11,762) and passing touchdowns (95) in school history. The Irish offense was explosive in 2005 and 2006. The 2005 team scored a school record 440 points. The Irish went 9–3 in 2005 and 10–3 in 2006.

Notre Dame struggled after Quinn left for the NFL. The team went just 16–21 in Weis's last three years, from 2007 to 2009. He was fired after the 2009 season.

FLOYD SETS RECORDS

Notre Dame has a history filled with great receivers. But Michael Floyd might be the best the Irish have ever had. He was a four-year starter from 2008 to 2011. Floyd set nearly every receiving record at Notre Dame. He finished with school records for career receptions (271), receiving yards (3,686), and touchdown catches (37). In 2011, Floyd had 1,147 yards on 100 catches, a school record for a single season.

Quarterback Brady Quinn led the Irish to a 10–3 record in 2006. Their previous 10-plus-win season was 2002.

The school hired former Cincinnati coach Brian Kelly to replace Weis in 2010. He brought a new sense of hope to the Irish, and he delivered early. The team started 1–3 in 2010. Yet the Irish finished 8–5 and won the Sun Bowl. Three of the five losses came by four points or less.

The winning continued in 2011. Notre Dame finished the regular season at 8–4. Despite a loss to Florida State in the Champs Sports Bowl, the Irish had back-to-back eight-win seasons for the first time in five years. Behind Kelly's leadership, the Irish and their fans looked to the future with hope that the glory days would soon return to South Bend.

TIMELINE

1887

On November 23, Notre Dame plays its first football game, losing to Michigan 8–0.

1920

Coach Knute Rockne and star player George Gipp lead the Irish to a second straight 9–0 season. Shortly after the season, Gipp dies after complications from strep throat.

1924

Led by the famed Four Horsemen backfield, the Irish win their first national title.

1929

Rockne and quarterback Frank Carideo guide the Irish to a second national title.

1930

Notre Dame Stadium is dedicated, and the Irish celebrate their new home in style. They finish 10–0 and win a second straight national title.

1953

John Lattner, who does a little of everything on the field for Notre Dame, becomes the school's fourth Heisman Trophy winner.

1956

Notre Dame struggles to a 2–8 season, but Paul Hornung is a star. Hornung wins the Heisman Trophy to become the first—and only—player from a losing team to win the award through 2011.

1964

A dramatic loss to Southern California is the only thing to prevent Notre Dame from a national title. The Irish get another Heisman Trophy winner, though, in John Huarte.

1966

A famous late-season tie with Michigan State helps Notre Dame stay at number one and win its eighth national title.

1973

Notre Dame finishes a perfect 11–0, including a one-point win over Alabama in the Sugar Bowl, to win its ninth national title.

1931

On March 31, Rockne is killed in a plane crash in Kansas. During his 13-year tenure as coach, the Irish went 105–12–5.

1943

Despite a loss in its last game, Notre Dame wins its fourth national championship, and its first with coach Frank Leahy. Quarterback Angelo Bertelli is the first Notre Dame player to win the Heisman Trophy.

1946

After missing the previous two seasons because of military service, Leahy returns to the team. He leads the Irish to their fifth national title.

1947

John Lujack wins Notre Dame's second Heisman Trophy. He also leads the Irish to their second straight national title.

1949

Leahy and the Irish win their third title in four years. Heisman Trophy winner Leon Hart leads the way.

1977

Future Pro Football Hall of Fame quarterback Joe Montana guides the Irish to their tenth national title.

1987

Receiver/kick returner Tim Brown becomes the seventh Heisman Trophy winner in Notre Dame history.

1988

Coach Lou Holtz and quarterback Tony Rice steer Notre Dame to a 12–0 record and the eleventh national championship in school history.

2006

Coach Charlie Weis and quarterback Brady Quinn lead the Irish to a 10–3 record. Their 19 combined wins for 2005 and 2006 is the team's most in a two-year stretch since winning 21 from 1992 to 1993.

2010

Brian Kelly is named the 29th coach in Notre Dame history. He leads the team to bowl games in each of his first two seasons.

QUICK STATS

PROGRAM INFO

University of Notre Dame Catholics, Hoosiers, Ramblers, Rockmen, Westerners (1887–1926)
University of Notre Dame Fighting Irish (1927–)

NATIONAL CHAMPIONSHIPS
(* DENOTES SHARED TITLE)

1924, 1929, 1930, 1943, 1946, 1947, 1949, 1966, 1973*, 1977, 1988

OTHER ACHIEVEMENTS

BCS bowl appearances (1999–): 3
Bowl record: 15–16

KEY PLAYERS
(POSITION[S]; SEASONS WITH TEAM)

Angelo Bertelli (QB; 1941–43) †
Tim Brown (WR; 1984–87) †
Ross Browner (DE; 1973, 1975–77)
George Connor (T; 1946–47)
Bob Crable (LB; 1979–81)
George Gipp (HB; 1917–20)
Leon Hart (E/DE; 1947–49) †
Paul Hornung (QB/S; 1954–56) †
John Huarte (QB; 1962–64) †
Raghib Ismail (WR; 1988–90)
John Lattner (HB; 1951–53) †
John Lujack (QB; 1943, 1946–47) †
Joe Montana (QB; 1975, 77–78)
Alan Page (DE; 1964–66)
Tony Rice (QB; 1987–89)

† denotes Heisman Trophy winner

KEY COACHES

Lou Holtz (1986–96): 100–30–2; 5–4 (bowl games)
Frank Leahy (1941–43, 1946–53): 87–11–9
Ara Parseghian (1967–74): 95–17–4; 3–2 (bowl games)
Knute Rockne (1918–30): 105–12–5; 1–0 (bowl games)

HOME STADIUM

Notre Dame Stadium (1930–)

* All statistics through 2011 season

QUOTES & ANECDOTES

Hesburgh Library sits just outside of Notre Dame Stadium. On the wall facing the stadium is a large mural of Jesus, surrounded by his followers. In the picture, Jesus is raising his arms—similar to how a referee would signal a touchdown. Although stadium expansion has largely blocked the view of the mural from inside, the mural will forever be known as "Touchdown Jesus."

The College Football Hall of Fame has a lot of Notre Dame flavor. As of 2011, 43 former Irish players and six former Notre Dame coaches were enshrined in the Hall of Fame. No other school in the country had more Hall of Famers.

"I've been in a Super Bowl and I've played in front of a hundred thousands fans, but nothing in my 12-year NFL career ever compared to running out on the field at Notre Dame Stadium. It felt like my feet never touched the ground. To this day, I still get goosebumps just talking about it." —Joe Theismann, Notre Dame quarterback, 1968 to 1970

Notre Dame has had seven Heisman Trophy winners. It has had a bunch of others come close, too. Beginning with Bill Shakespeare, who was third in the original voting in 1935, the Irish have had 28 players finish in the top five of the Heisman voting through 2011. Angelo Bertelli (1941), Joe Theismann (1970), and Raghib Ismail (1990) all finished second. Bertelli won the award in 1943.

GLOSSARY

All-American
A player chosen as one of the best amateurs in the country in a particular activity.

calamity
A disaster.

consensus
Unanimous agreement.

draft
A system used by professional sports leagues to select new players in order to spread incoming talent among all teams. The NFL Draft is held each spring.

inducted
To be ceremoniously admitted to a position or place, such as the Hall of Fame.

legend
An extremely famous person, especially in a particular field.

rankings
A system where voters rank the best teams in the country.

rival
An opponent that brings out great emotion in a team, its fans, and its players.

two-point conversion
To complete a two-point conversion a team has one opportunity to get the ball into the end zone on the play immediately after scoring a touchdown.

upset
A result where the supposedly worse team defeats the supposedly better team.

FOR MORE INFORMATION

FURTHER READING

Green, David. *101 Reasons to Love Notre Dame Football*, New York: Stewart, Tabori & Chang, 2009.

Heisler, John. *100 Things Notre Dame Fans Should Know & Do Before They Die*, Chicago: Triumph Books, 2009.

Heisler, John. *Greatest Moments in Notre Dame Football History*, Chicago: Triumph Books, 2008.

WEB LINKS

To learn more about the Notre Dame Fighting Irish, visit ABDO Publishing Company online at **www.abdopublishing.com**. Web sites about the Fighting Irish are featured on our Book Links page. These links are routinely monitored and updated to provide the most current information available.

PLACES TO VISIT

College Football Hall of Fame
111 South St. Joseph St.
South Bend, IN 46601
1-800-440-FAME (3263)
www.collegefootball.org

This hall of fame and museum highlights the greatest players and moments in the history of college football. Among the former Fighting Irish enshrined here are Knute Rockne, George Gipp, Paul Hornung, Alan Page, and Tim Brown.

Notre Dame Stadium
Edison Road & Juniper Road
South Bend, IN 46600
219-631-7246
www.und.com/facilities/nd-stadium.html

This has been Notre Dame's home field since 1930. The Irish have sold out all but one game here since 1966.

ABOUT THE AUTHOR

Brian Howell is a freelance writer based in Denver, Colorado. He has been a sports journalist for nearly 20 years, writing about high school, college, and professional athletics. In addition, he has written books about sports and history. A native of Colorado, he lives with his wife and four children in his home state.